CHRISTOPHER CHURCHMOUSE CLASSICS®

A CHURCHMOUSE CHRISTMAS

"Thank God for His son — His Gift too wonderful for words."
— 2 Corinthians 9:15 (THE LIVING BIBLE)

WRITTEN BY BARBARA DAVOLL
Pictures by Dennis Hockerman

VICTOR BOOKS

A DIVISION OF SCRIPTURE PRESS PUBLICATIONS INC.
USA CANADA ENGLAND

CHRISTOPHER CHURCHMOUSE CLASSICS

Saved by the Bell
The White Trail
A Sunday Surprise
The Potluck Supper
The Tattletale Tongue
A Flood of Friends
A Load of Trouble
Rainy Day Rescue

A Pack of Lies
The Shiny Red Sled
A Sticky Mystery
A Short Tail
Grandpa's Secret
The Camping Caper
A Churchmouse Birthday

**ALSO AVAILABLE—*A Churchmouse Christmas:
A Musical for Children***

This delightful children's musical was written by Barbara Davoll and Don Wyrtzen for children ages 5–10. With 8 songs and a timeless message, it brings Christopher Churchmouse to life in a brand new way. Look for these related products produced by Lillenas Publishing Company and available through your local Christian bookstore:

A Churchmouse Christmas (music and lyrics)/MC-88
Stereo Cassette/TA-9173C
Choral Promo Pack/L-9173C
Accompaniment Cassette/MU-9173C
Accompaniment Compact Disc/MU-9173T
Performance Manual/MC-88A
Multimedia Slide Set/MM-9173
Service Folders/MC-88SF

Scripture quotations are from *The Living Bible*, © 1971,
Tyndale House Publishers, Wheaton, IL 60189.
Used by permission.

4 5 6 7 8 9 10 Printing/Year 98 97 96 95

VICTOR BOOKS
A division of SP Publications, Inc.
Wheaton, IL 60187

A WORD TO PARENTS AND TEACHERS

The Christopher Churchmouse Classics
will please both the eyes and ears of children and
help them grow in the knowledge of God.

This book, *A Churchmouse Christmas,*
one of the character-building stories in the series,
is about the real meaning of our Christmas giving.

"Thank God for His Son — His gift too wonderful for words."
—2 Corinthians 9:15 (THE LIVING BIBLE)

Through this story about Christopher,
children will see a practical application of this Bible truth.

Happy reading!

Christopher's Friend,

Barbara Davoll

"Twas the night before Christmas and all through the church-house,
Not a creature was stirring — but Christopher Churchmouse.
The old church was quiet, no sound was there made;
The mice had returned from their nightly church raid.

Mama and Papa were snug in their beds,
While dreams of mice-krispies now danced in their heads.
Little baby churchmouse, like a bug in a rug,
Was curled up in her nutshell, cozy and snug.

Across from Mouse Manor slept Snootie and Rootie,
In canopy beds of luxurious beauty.
And Christopher's cousins, Sed, Ted, and Ned,
Were all soundly sleeping, warm and well-fed.

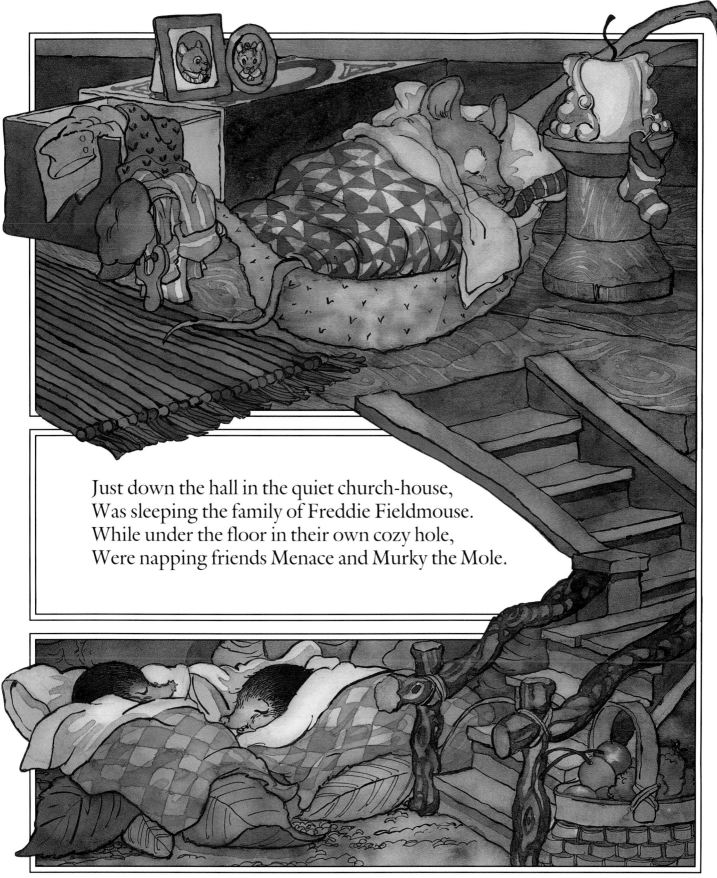

Just down the hall in the quiet church-house,
Was sleeping the family of Freddie Fieldmouse.
While under the floor in their own cozy hole,
Were napping friends Menace and Murky the Mole.

Tuffy was sleeping in his usual place,
Curled up by the furnace in a cozy, warm space.

And across the hall in her little home handy
Was Christopher's own special friend, Mandy.

Tucked way out of sight in a house full of junk,
Dozed Peter the Packrat in his messy bunk.
Grandpa and grandma were snoring and sleeping.
The clock on their wall a long vigil was keeping.

In all of the church only Chris was awake,
And although excited, no sound did he make.
With an eye on the clock, he awaited his cue,
For he still had something important to do.

A few weeks ago he had heard Preacher say
That soon they would celebrate Jesus' birthday.
Christmas, he'd said, was when God sent His Son,
So people could know of this WONDERFUL ONE.
He'd further explained that Christmas meant love,
For Jesus had come from heaven above.
That Jesus had come was clearly the reason
So much attention was given the season.

As Christmas drew closer the people grew busy;
Just watching them work had made Christopher dizzy.
One day Chris had watched from his own special perch,
And saw the people as they trimmed the church.
They had set up a scene of a manger with hay
With people and animals all made of clay.

That day Chris noticed just one thing was lacking.
There was no churchmouse that they were unpacking.
He had promptly decided right then and there,
They needed a mouse; it would only be fair.
If sheep, cows, and donkeys and camels and such
Could all gather there, would a mouse be too much?

For weeks now Chris had been carving some wood,
And making a churchmouse as fine as he could.

When he had finished the tiny wood mouse,
And hid it away in his own little house,

He marked off the days till the moment was right
So he could deliver his gift on this night.
He'd eagerly waited until Christmas Eve,
Not thinking at all of the gifts he'd receive.

Instead he'd been thinking and planning the way
He'd deliver his gift before Christmas Day.
So carefully waiting till all were asleep;
Till no eye was open, not even a peep.

With a shiver of joy and a smile ear to.ear,
Christopher knew that the time was now here.
Secretly Chris left his hole in the wall;
The tiny carved mouse was clutched in his paw.
Now softly tiptoeing down the church aisle,
The little mouse felt it must be a mile.

Coming at last to the front of the church,
Christopher stared and stopped with a lurch.
A soft light shone down on a manger with hay,
Where lay Baby Jesus, a doll made of clay.

"Happy Birthday," squeaked Christopher. "This is for You."
His whisper was soft, yet it reached the back pew.
Then placing his mouse in the scene on the floor,
And turning around, he ran straight out the door.

Back to Mouse Manor the little mouse sped,
Blew out his candle, then hopped into bed.
His gift was delivered, the secret he'd keep.
A smile on his face, he was soon fast asleep.

When Christopher wakened, the church bell was ringing.
He knew he was late; the people were singing.

When he was all dressed and at last in his place,
The joy he was feeling now shone on his face.
Chris was so happy that bright Christmas Day,
He sang out with joy in the merriest way.

For right there in front of the beautiful church
Was the mouse he had carved from a small piece of birch.
Christopher knew that he'd done what he could,
For even a churchmouse can do what he should.

Although it may seem he had just a small part,
Chris knew that a mouse can't give Jesus his heart.
For that's something only REAL people can do —
Like mommies and daddies and small folk like you.

So while you are thinking about His birthday,
What will you give Him, and what will you say?
"Dear Jesus, I love You and I'll give You my heart."
By doing just that you'll have done the best part.

23

A Churchmouse Christmas

Barbara Davoll

Don Wyrtzen

1. A church-mouse Christ-mas! The best time of the year!____
2. (A) church-mouse Christ-mas! And ev-'ry-thing's brand new!____

Chil-ly cheeks and fros-ty toes,____ Look out-side, I hope it snows,____
Can-dles shin-ing in the night,____ Christ-mas cook-ies, want a bite?____

Burst-ing with a joy that glows And with Christ-mas good cheer.____ A
Mis-tle-toe hangs out of sight, Mer-ry Christ-mas to you!____ A

Church-mouse Christ-mas! The best time of the year!____
Church-mouse Christ-mas! And ev-'ry-thing's brand new!____

Shake and rat-tle, who's it for?____ Whis-pers heard be-hind the door,____
Toss and turn, I'm wide a-wake,____ Time is near, there's no mis-take,____

What sur-pris-es are in store as we lis-ten and hear!
Sea-son's here so cel-e-brate! Mer-ry

2. A

Christ-mas, to you, A mer-ry Church-mouse to me; A mer-ry

Chris-mouse to you____ and____ me!____ *Wheee!*